THE LOST
WORLD

MADARA
THE MIDNIGHT
WARRIOR

With special thanks to Allan Frewin Jones

For Martha and Monty

www.beastquest.co.uk

ORCHARD BOOKS
338 Euston Road, London NW1 3BH
Orchard Books Australia
Level 17/207 Kent St, Sydney, NSW 2000

A Paperback Original
First published in Great Britain in 2010

Beast Quest is a registered trademark of Beast Quest Limited
Series created by Working Partners Limited, London

Text © Beast Quest Limited 2010
Cover and inside illustrations by Steve Sims © Orchard Books 2010

A CIP catalogue record for this book is available from
the British Library.

ISBN 978 1 40830 732 8

Printed and bound in China by Imago

The paper and board used in this paperback are natural recyclable
products made from wood grown in sustainable forests. The
manufacturing processes conform to the environmental regulations of
the country of origin.

Orchard Books is a division of Hachette Children's Books,
an Hachette UK company

www.hachette.co.uk

MADARA
THE MIDNIGHT
WARRIOR

BY ADAM BLADE

ORCHARD BOOKS

THE FOREST
OF DOOM

SOUTHERN RIVER

THE
SCARLET
DESERT

Welcome to another world, where Dark Forces are at play.

Tom thought he was on his way back home; he was wrong. My son has entered another realm where nothing is as it seems. Six monstrous Beasts threaten all corners of the kingdom, and Tom and Elenna must face an enemy they thought long gone. I have never been so proud of my son, but can he be all that I always hoped he would be? Or shall a mother watch her son fail?

One question remains. Are you brave enough to join Tom on the most deadly Quest yet?

Only you know the answer...

Freya, Mistress of the Beasts

PROLOGUE

Jude grinned as he crept towards the cattle pen. He could hear the cows moving about nervously inside. He glanced up at the Tavanian night. Ripples of colour moved around a long dark slash in the sky. The patterns glowed with an eerie light.

"No wonder the cows are restless," he muttered. He looked away, concentrating on the task at hand.

Usually, the cattle pen's gate would be under constant guard. But Malvel had called all able-bodied men to join his army. Now, the countryside had emptied out nicely! Nicely if, like Jude, you were a thief.

"Come to Jude," he whispered, opening the gate. "Come and make me some easy money."

He slipped inside, smelling the animals all around him, hearing the thud of their hooves on the ground. The cows jostled against one another as he walked among them, running his hand over their flanks.

Finally, he slapped the haunch of a cow. "You'll do, my sturdy friend."

A moment later he had slipped a noose around the animal's neck and was leading it out of the herd.

He walked the cow out of the pen and closed the gate. But as he began to lead his four-legged prize towards his horse, he stopped. His ears pricked up at a strange sound: a low growl.

Then a second growl sounded out of the darkness, deep and resonant. Jude bit his lip and shivered. The cow snorted and rolled its eyes, fretfully pulling on the noose.

"Steady," Jude said, but his voice was trembling. He pulled the cow to his tethered horse, over by a tree. Quickly mounting, Jude tied the end of the noose rope around the saddle pommel. He spurred his horse into a gentle trot, pulling the cow with him.

"We've done well tonight, my friend," Jude said, patting his horse's neck. "Plenty of meat for the butcher. Why, we'll feed on the profits for—"

Another eerie growl stopped the words in his throat.

His horse faltered, tossing his mane nervously. The cow lowed and dragged back on the rope, the bell around its neck jingling. The sound was closer this time – much closer.

Jude peered into the night, wishing he had brought a weapon. What was following him like a shadow?

Out of the corner of his eye, he saw a flash of white. He turned his head, but there was nothing to see. Fear crawled up his spine like icy fingers.

"Who's there?" he called.

He dug his heels into the horse's flanks, urging it to quicken its pace. The rope went taut as the cow was pulled along. The growling seemed much closer now.

He almost considered cutting the cow loose and kicking his horse to a gallop. *I need to get away!*

There was the sound of paws padding on the hard earth.

Something was close by, moving quickly. The cow lowed, a panicky sound. He stared back the way they had come. Two lights hung in the air, flashing like twinkling coins.

Eyes!

But if they were eyes, they were too far above the ground – what kind of creature could be so large?

"Quick!" Jude urged his horse.

But a heartbeat later the rope holding the cow went taut, thrumming like a bowstring. Jude felt his horse being pulled backwards, the tight rope cutting hard against his thigh, almost dragging him out of the saddle. He could hear dreadful sounds behind him – the cow's desperate bellows shredding the

night. Something tugged hard on the rope, the cow lowed pitifully one final time, and then a loud squelching sound made Jude want to be sick. The rope went slack.

Horrified, Jude reeled it in. The end was frayed and bloodstained. He kicked his horse's flanks. The horse lurched forwards.

Then he saw that white shape again, at the very edge of sight. He turned his head in terror as the whiteness came leaping towards him. He let out a yell. Two lidless eyes that glittered with rage. Fur glistening like white crystals. Long, sharp fangs and jet-black claws like scythes.

His horse put on a spurt of speed and for a moment Jude thought they would pass safely in front of the leaping monster. He ducked, crying out in agony as he felt the claws rake his back, slicing through flesh.

But that frantic burst of speed from his horse had saved him. He clung close to his horse's neck, wrapping the reins around his wrists, his back throbbing and dripping with blood.

Almost fainting with pain, he leaned forwards. "Get us home!"

As the horse galloped away, Jude swayed forward in the saddle and the world around him went black.

CHAPTER ONE

THE DEADLY PORTAL

Tom wiped his sleeve across his forehead. The battle with Krestor had exhausted him, but he had no time to rest – a new challenge awaited. He glanced down at his sword, the blade burned away by Krestor's acid.

Storm, Tom's noble stallion, picked his way down the mountainside. Silver, Elenna's wolf, was loping from boulder to boulder, his grey body low to the ground, yellow eyes shining.

Tom turned to look at Elenna, sitting behind him on Storm's back. She was scanning the tumbling foothills that led to a vast open plain.

"I have to keep reminding myself that we're not in Avantia," she commented.

Tom knew what she meant. Tavania was similar to their homeland, yet also very different. Portals had been torn open in the glassy dome that covered the kingdom. Beasts had been sucked up into the tears in the sky and scattered across Tavania, far from their natural homes. Now they were confused and very dangerous.

Worse than this, Tom's enemy, Malvel, rules Tavania. Only by defeating the Beasts in battle can

Tom restore good King Henri to the throne and restore balance to the kingdom. Only then could he defeat Malvel.

But with Tom and Elenna's help, the kingdom's Good Wizard Oradu was gradually becoming stronger. Tom had already defeated three Beasts, and with each victory one of Oradu's magical possessions was returned to him: a cloak, a hat and, most recently, the wizard's staff. When his possessions are returned to him, Oradu would have the strength to take on Malvel in combat.

Oradu had already told them the name of the next Beast they must find: Madara.

But where was the Beast lurking?

Tom drew his magical map out of the folds of his shirt. He had found it in his saddlebag at the start of this Quest, put there by Oradu, and so far it had always shown him the right way to go.

He unfolded the small gold panels, feeling the fine metal cold under his fingers. A pathway of shining amber would lead them to the next Beast. But before any path appeared, Elenna's hand clutched his shoulder.

"I don't think we need the map this time," she said. "Look!"

She pointed out over the foothills to where the wide plains of Tavania stretched away. The sun was low in the sky. Afternoon was giving way to evening. Long shadows spun out over the landscape, spindly and sinister.

Against the huge dome of the darkening sky, Tom saw a new portal.

It was like a long dark wound
hanging in the air. Red and purple
clouds rolled and swirled around
the slit, stabbed through by bolts
of violent lightning – yellow, blue
and green.

"We need to get there quickly,"

Tom said, snapping the reins to send Storm down through the foothills at a wild gallop. Elenna clung on behind. Panting with excitement, Silver raced along at their side.

They came out onto the plain, clods of earth and tufts of grass flying in their wake as Storm thundered out over the rugged, hilly landscape. Tom stared up at the ugly gash as it twisted and spiralled against the darkening sky.

He reined Storm in as they came closer to the portal. A powerful wind howled across the plain, so strong that it was all Tom could do not to be plucked out of the saddle.

"This is not a natural storm," Elenna called. "Malvel's turning the land against us again!"

Tom nodded. Malvel's hold over

Tavania was so strong he could attack his enemies with earth and water – and now wind.

"We need to get down," Tom shouted to Elenna. "We'll use Storm as cover."

They slipped off Storm's back and huddled together against his side. Still they felt the vicious whip of the wind lashing their skin. The dreadful howling got louder. Storm stumbled a pace or two. Silver came slinking close, low to the ground, his fur rippling and his ears back as he bared his teeth, barking and snarling.

Tom tried to see what was making the wolf so angry.

Through the whirl of the wind, something was approaching, bearing down on them at a terrible speed.

CHAPTER TWO

THE EYE OF THE STORM

Tom threw himself out of the
way as a great ball of tumbleweed
went hurtling past, driven by the
howling wind.

"Watch out!" yelled Elenna as he
scrambled to his feet.

A second ball of tumbleweed came
spinning on the wind, driving him to
his knees.

Tom gritted his teeth against the pain. This was no ordinary tumbleweed – the racing and whirling ball was threaded with thorns. They had torn his clothes and raked his skin, drawing blood.

Storm whinnied in alarm as a third ball of thorns slammed into Tom, driving him to the ground, ripping

through his clothes.

And there were more – scores of the deadly balls flung themselves at Tom and his friends. Howling and snapping at the air, Silver threw himself from side to side to avoid them. Storm reared up, his forelegs wheeling and his eyes rolling in fear.

"Over here!" Tom could only just hear Elenna's voice over the roaring wind and the hissing, crackling tumbleweeds. Keeping flat to the ground, he turned his head, trying to see her.

Her arm lifted from a hollow in the ground, frantically waving.

"I'm coming!" Tom shouted.

He leapt towards Storm, giving him a solid whack on the rump to drive him safely out of the path of the tumbleweeds.

Keeping an arm up over his face, Tom threw himself into the shallow ditch where Elenna had found refuge. It was only large enough for the two of them.

"Silver! Get away from here! Follow Storm to safety." Elenna shouted. The wolf gave a howl and scampered away.

"This is Malvel's work, for sure," gasped Tom. "He's setting the land against us, just like he did with the river and the rock falls in the mountains."

"What can we do against his magic?" Elenna shouted, above the wailing wind.

Tom huddled in the ditch. "Nothing right now," he said. "We'll just have to wait."

For a long time the vicious

tumbleweeds kept on coming and the wind kept roaring. Worry for his animal companions gnawed at Tom's insides as the sky slowly faded.

Would this attack never end? Elenna and Tom looked anxiously at one another as evening slowly turned to night. Still the tumbleweeds rushed by, thrown towards them by Malvel's evil gusts of wind.

Then, quite suddenly, the wind died down.

Tom leaped to his feet, shaking his fists at the sky. "Hear me, Malvel!" he shouted. "While there is blood in my veins, you shall not stop me!"

Tom almost expected some sign of anger from the wizard, but there was just the eerie silence of the rugged plain, and the endless writhing of the portal in the sky.

From the settling clouds of dust, Storm and Silver trotted over to them. Tom had some rips in his clothes, and there was a little blood from the long narrow cuts, but the thorns had not dug in deeply.

"Are you alright?" Tom asked as Elenna brushed the dirt from her clothes.

She shrugged. "I am now that storm has stopped. Come on, let's get going."

They mounted Storm and went trotting further across the hilly plain. Their way was lit by the eerie glow of the lightning flickering at the portal's edges.They were coming closer to the tear in the sky now. The clouds surrounding it hung over their heads, and forked lightning stabbed down at the ground.

"Is it a good idea to ride into the storm at night?" asked Elenna.

"Probably not," Tom said. "But we've never walked away from danger before – and I'm not about to start now." He looked at her. "The Beasts have always been near these tears in the sky. Madara will be somewhere close by, for sure. Are you ready to fight?"

"Of course!" said Elenna.

They rode on towards the storm. Thunder growled and the lightning sent down its shining darts. There was no rain.

"Halt! Who goes there?"

Two figures stood on a ridge of land, clearly visible in the starlight – soldiers, judging by their armour.

They jumped down from the ridge and approached, lowering long pikes.

"Dismount your horse," demanded the first man, turning the barbed point of his pike towards Silver, who was snarling and bearing his teeth. "Control that mutt!"

"Steady, Silver," said Elenna.

Tom was thinking fast. His only weapon was his damaged sword – that would be no defence against two armed soldiers.

"Do as they say," Tom whispered to Elenna. "But at my signal, call Silver to attack."

"No talking there!" shouted the first man. "Nathan, tie them up."

"Get down," said the second man. "Do as we say and you'll come to no harm."

Tom and Elenna dismounted.

"Quiet, boy," Tom murmured to his horse.

"Keep a close guard on them, Peter," said Nathan.

Peter aimed his pike at the two friends. "I will. Make sure those knots are tight! Think of the reward Malvel will give us for capturing the most wanted fugitives in Tavania!"

Tom glared at the man – so, these two knew who they were!

Nathan came closer, holding the rope between his hands.

"Now!" Tom hissed to Elenna.

She turned to Silver and gave a shrill whistle.

Understanding what was wanted of him, Silver sprang forwards, closing

his jaws over Peter's arm.

Nathan spun around at the other man's cry of pain. Quick as a whip, Tom drew his broken sword and brought the hilt down hard on the back of Nathan's skull.

Nathan fell on all fours, dropping his pike.

Tom stooped to retrieve the weapon while Elenna ran to where Silver held Peter secure. She held out her hand. Wincing from the pain of the wolf's teeth in his arm, Peter dropped the pike into her grip.

Tom gave the two soldiers a grim look. "Do as we say!" he said. "Don't try anything stupid."

CHAPTER THREE

A THOUSAND FOES

"Have mercy!" cried Peter. "We're just a scouting party. We wouldn't have really hurt you."

"You would have handed us over to Malvel," Tom said. "Do you think he would have shown us mercy?"

The man licked his lips nervously.

"You needn't worry," Tom said. "We're not cold blooded murderers. Elenna, call Silver off."

His friend gave a whistle and the wolf released Peter, who fell back, rubbing his arm.

Nathan got slowly to his feet, his hand to the back of his head where Tom had struck him. "Malvel has a whole army hunting you," he snarled. "There's no escape."

"Show us this so-called army!" demanded Elenna.

The man gave a crooked grin. He pointed to a long ridge of high ground. "See for yourself."

"Keep them under guard!" Tom said to Elenna as he climbed the ridge. She trained her bow on the men, an arrow fitted on the string. Silver sat next to her and growled.

Tom scrambled to the top, careful not to lose his footing in the gloom. The sight that met his eyes made his heart pound in his chest.

Under the eerie shifting lights of the portal, the plain was alive with soldiers. Tom dropped to his belly so that he could not be seen.

Fortunately, even the closest of the soldiers was a good way out on the plain. But there were hundreds of them, all bristling with weaponry – and all marching towards the portal.

He crawled to the back of the ridge and gestured for Elenna to join him.

While Silver kept watch on the two men, Tom quickly told his friend what he had seen.

"But how will we find the Beast?" she asked, keeping her voice low. "If Madara is lurking close to the portal, we'd have to pass through the entire army to get to it."

Tom was thinking hard. "We can't outrun the army, and we can't avoid them – but perhaps we can join them."

Elenna gave him a puzzled look. "The moment they see us, we'll be captured and sent to Malvel," she hissed urgently.

"That won't happen if the soldiers don't realize who we are," Tom explained. He pointed to Nathan and Peter. "Their clothes and helmets will be big, but in the night, I think there's a good chance we'll be able to slip in alongside the other soldiers without raising suspicion. And as soon as we can, we'll get ahead of them and find the Beast."

"What about Storm and Silver?" she asked. "There's no way to disguise them."

"We can say we captured them," said Tom.

"Good thinking," she said. Then she frowned. "Except that I hardly look like a man. Wait!" She rubbed her hands in the dirt then smeared it over her face. "Do I look more convincing, now?"

She peered at him with bright eyes through the grimy mask. With her short hair and lithe build, she looked like a young boy-recruit in Malvel's army.

"Yes, you do," said Tom, smiling. "Now let's complete the disguises."

The two friends climbed down to where Storm and Silver stood over the men.

"We'll be needing your clothes," Tom ordered.

The men hesitated, and then began peeling off their mail vests and helmets. Soon, they stood shivering in their long underwear. Peter was a little shorter and slighter than Nathan, so Elenna dressed in his clothes while Tom put on Nathan's.

The mail vest was uncomfortable,
and the helmet weighed down
heavily on his head.

"You won't get far," scoffed Nathan.

"We'll see," Tom replied.

He and Elenna used the men's own
rope to tie their hands and feet.

Then Tom found some old rags in his saddlebag to use as gags. Nathan glared at him as he wound a rag around his mouth. Tom didn't like treating them this badly, but he couldn't risk them calling to their comrades.

"I'm sure someone will find you before too long," Tom told them. He turned to Elenna. "We'd better not ride Storm," he said. "We should put leashes on him and Silver – that way they'll be more convincing as our prisoners."

Leaving the two soldiers tied and gagged, Tom and Elenna led their animal friends around the ridge and out onto the plain.

Far ahead, they could see that the army was setting up camp for the night. Clusters of red tents were being erected across the plain and fires were being lit.

"He really doesn't like this," said Elenna, looking anxiously at Silver. The wolf was jerking at the rope, twisting his neck as though trying to bite through it.

Tom patted Storm's neck. "It's for the best," he tried to explain. "No harm will come to you, I promise."

The four companions moved onwards towards the nearest camp. Tom could see men crowded around a fire, their swords and armour glinting in the flames.

Tom peered out from under his borrowed helmet.

I hope these disguises fool them, he thought, his heart beating hard in his chest. *If not, we're walking right into Malvel's hands!*

CHAPTER FOUR

SURROUNDED!

A sentry marched up to them, his pike at the ready. "Who are you?" he demanded.

"A scouting party," Tom replied, making his voice a deep growl. "My name is Nathan and this is Peter."

The sentry peered at them. "Where did you find those animals? They look like the horse and the wolf that travel with the fugitives."

"So they should," Elenna said gruffly. "We came upon the fugitives, and they fled from us, leaving them both behind."

"A cowardly trick," declared the sentry. "So much for the bond between the girl and her wolf!"

Tom saw Elenna's shoulders stiffen with silent anger.

"You've done well," said the sentry, clapping a hand on Tom's back. "Without the horse, they won't be able to outrun us for long. Which way did they go?"

Tom turned and pointed, avoiding the direction from which they had come. He didn't want the real Nathan and Peter to be found. Not yet, anyway.

"I'll have a detachment sent after them," said the sentry. "You deserve a meal and some rest. Tie up those animals and sit by the fire."

"We'll do that," said Tom. "Hope you find the fugitives."

Tom and Elenna led Storm and Silver into the camp of their enemies.

"You did well," whispered Tom.

"So did you," Elenna replied. She looked regretfully at Silver. "I only hope our friends can be patient."

"They know we'll never let them come to harm," said Tom.

They arrived at the crackling fire, where most of the soldiers now sat.

"Well done, friends!" called out a soldier.

"Capturing those animals was a great deed!" said another. "Tether them to stakes and come join us!"

Storm and Silver were tied to stakes hammered into the ground. Tom and

Elenna sat close to the fire. Many men were huddled around the flames; as the night deepened, chilly winds were moving over the plains. The faces of the men looked gloomy in the flickering firelight. Some of them had chain mail that glittered as they moved; others wore breastplates that glowed red in the flames.

To the east, the restless lightning flashed and crackled from the seething clouds that surrounded the portal.

A huge cauldron hung over the fire. A man was skinning and quartering rabbits that he threw into the bubbling vegetable stew.

"You seem very young to be in Malvel's army," remarked a man sitting close by.

"We've only just enlisted," Tom replied, hoping their disguises would work. "We're not too young to fight."

"Brave words," laughed another man. "And where do you both hail from?"

"Wherever they come from, they're on the same fool's errand as all of us," interrupted one of the soldiers.

Tom looked at the man in surprise.

"Be silent!" snapped another soldier, looking over his shoulder. "Don't talk like that, or there'll be trouble!"

"What more trouble could Tavania be in?" exclaimed the first speaker. "Malvel claims to be the kingdom's saviour, but I'm not so sure. I want King Henri back on the throne!"

Tom felt Elenna's hand on his arm. When he looked round he could see that she was listening intently.

"He's right," said another man, shooting a glance up at the troubled sky. "I remember a time when our kingdom wasn't plagued by these fearsome rips in the heavens."

"Aye," added the first man. "And it's said that dreadful monsters fall from those holes, devouring everything that crosses their paths."

"Be silent, you superstitious fools!" demanded an officer, as he passed by. "The next man speaking such nonsense will be thrown in the dungeons!"

He strode off, leaving the men muttering to each other.

"At the very least, this army provides us with a living," said the man seated next to Tom. He shook his head. "I don't know how my son, Jude, is managing to survive with no wages for food."

"It's not much better here," said one of the men. "Just dry bread and scrawny rabbits. My stomach is growling like a wolf!"

"Speaking of wolves," said another, turning to where Storm and Silver were tethered. "I'd say there's a fair bit of meat on those two animals."

More heads turned, hungry eyes glinting in the dark.

"Plenty of meat!" said another of the men, drawing his sword and rising from the fireside. "Who's for a real feast, lads? Horse and wolf meat will go down a treat!"

Tom stared at the man in alarm. Did Malvel's soldiers really mean to kill Storm and Silver?

CHAPTER FIVE

THE MENACING SHADOW

Elenna sprang up. "We'd be fools to butcher these animals," she exclaimed in a gruff voice. "If we keep them alive, we can use them to lure the fugitives in."

"Would you let greed ruin a good chance of using the animals as bait?" Tom added. "What would Malvel think of that?"

The man with the drawn sword strode towards the animals. "I want meat now!" he snarled. "I'm sick of being hungry all the time."

Tom caught him by the arm.

"No! You can't do that!" he said, glaring into the man's face.

"They have a point, Brant," said another of the soldiers. "Let's be content with rabbit tonight. We can look forward to better meat tomorrow, when the boy and the girl are found."

For a moment, Brant stared angrily at Tom, and then he sheathed his sword and sat down again. Tom and Elenna returned to the fire. The difficult moment was over.

Everyone settled down again. Tom leaned close to Elenna. "We have to get out of here," he whispered.

"It's too dangerous."

Elenna nodded. "I have an idea," she whispered back.

"The food's ready," said the man who had been tossing the pieces of rabbit into the cauldron. He dipped a large ladle and took a sip of the steaming stew. He grimaced. "It's as bland as ditchwater, but it'll have to do." He gestured to a pile of flat loaves close to the fire. "There's plenty of bread to soak it up."

"Wait a moment," Elenna said. "I never travel without a few dried herbs for the pot."

She pulled out some small cloth bags and opened them, quickly gathering a mixture of aromatic herbs together.

"Well done, lad!" said the cook. "That's exactly what's needed!"

Elenna stood up and tossed the herbs into the stew. "Mix them in well," she said, "so that everyone gets the benefit!"

She sat down again, winking at Tom. "Don't eat the stew!" she whispered.

When the food was dished up, Tom and Elenna leaned in close over their bowls, pretending to eat as ravenously as the others were. The enticing smell of the herbs stole out over the camp, and soon there was a queue of men with bowls.

Now all Tom and Elenna had to do was wait.

It was not long before the man at Tom's side slumped sideways. Elenna had created a powerful sleeping draught!

More and more soldiers began

falling asleep, until the night was full of the sound of their snoring.

Tom looked around cautiously. Every soldier in the camp seemed to have succumbed. Further away on the plain, there were other cooking fires and more camps, but Tom felt sure that they could slip past them without being spotted.

They got up from the fire and made their way quietly to where Storm and Silver were tethered.

"Not a sound!" Elenna warned the wolf, putting a finger to her lips.

Although the animals were clearly pleased to be free again, neither of them made any noise. Tom quickly took some water flasks from the sleeping soldiers and snatched up a couple of loaves.

"What about weapons?" Elenna asked.

"Good idea." Tom took a spear while Elenna picked out a sword and a shield. "At least now we'll be armed to face the Beast when we find it."

Tom walked Storm to the edge of the camp with Elenna and Silver moving silently at their side.

Once they were sure that they were a safe distance from the dozing soldiers, they mounted Storm.

"Go!" Tom cried, and they went racing across the plains.

It was not long before they came to open and empty countryside.

We've evaded Malvel's army, Tom thought. *Now to find the Beast and complete our mission!* Above them, the night sky still glowed and flashed with the portal-lights.

"What's that ahead of us?" Tom wondered aloud as a burst of lightning lit up a curious, man-made structure in the valley ahead.

"I'm not sure," said Elenna, blinking as the lightning dazzled her eyes. "Is it a cattle pen?"

As they came closer, Tom saw that she was right.

But the sight that met their eyes was horrible. Some of the fences had been broken down, and the ground was scattered with the blood-soaked corpses of dozens of fallen cattle.

Storm stamped his hooves in alarm. Silver sniffed the air, growling uneasily, as though he could smell something menacing in the night.

"This is terrible," gasped Elenna, as they rode among the dead cows. "They haven't even been killed for food. What kind of a Beast would bring all this death just for the sake of it?"

"I don't know," said Tom, gripping his spear. "But whatever it is, our task is to hunt it down."

Leaving the carnage behind in the night, they came to a low ridge of land. Along the top stood a curious collection of standing stones, carved and shaped by wind and rain so that they almost resembled motionless people, staring silently out over the plain.

Tom shivered. Under the flaring bright light of the portal, the stones seemed to be watching them as they rode past.

Silver whined softly.

"Something moved!" Tom hissed. He gripped Elenna's wrist, pointing with his spear. "See?"

A shape was flitting from stone to stone.

"Should we find out what that is?" whispered Elenna.

Tom nodded. "We'll approach from opposite sides," he said. "That way it won't be able to escape."

Readying her sword and shield, Elenna slipped down from behind him and padded away across the face of the ridge.

Tom urged Storm up the slope towards the huddle of stones, clutching his spear in the crook of his arm.

He could still see the gliding shape; no more than a menacing shadow as

66

it slipped from cover to cover.

"Go!" said Tom, digging his heels into Storm's flanks.

With a whinny, the stallion galloped up the slope. At the last moment, Storm came to a clattering halt. Tom leaped from the saddle and ran among the stones.

Elenna came charging in from the left, her sword held high. Tom heard the terrified snort of an animal and a flash of lightning lifted the veil of darkness for just a second. Tom hesitated, with his spear held over his shoulder. A horse was crashing through the standing stones!

"There's a rider on the horse's back," Elenna called out. "I think he's hurt!"

CHAPTER SIX

THE WOUNDED STRANGER

Tom threw down his spear and ran towards the horse. The frightened animal reared up, but Tom sidestepped the thrashing hooves and managed to snatch hold of the bridle.

"Steady!" Tom crooned as the horse backed away. "You're safe now."

Soothed by his words, the horse calmed down. Elenna ran up, her

sword pushed into her belt. The rider
was lying over the horse's neck.

"Try to help him down," Tom said.

"The reins are tied around his
hands," Elenna said, working
frantically to get the knots loose.

With Tom's help, they managed to free the wounded youth and gently draw him down out of the saddle. They laid him carefully on his side. Tom and Elenna gasped when they saw that the back of his tunic had been torn to ribbons. Three deep, bloody gashes ran the length of his back.

As he lay shivering, they saw that his lips were moving.

"What's he saying?" asked Elenna.

Tom held his ear close to the young man's lips. "I don't know. I can't make anything out," he said. "Fetch some water from my saddlebag – and bread as well – he may be able to eat."

Tom looked closely into the youth's face. His skin was deathly pale. The wounds were terrible. Would he even survive the night? Ragged strips of his tunic had stuck to the drying blood on his back. Very carefully, Tom peeled the cloth away, the blood staining his hands as he did so.

As Elenna tended to the youth's wounds, Tom soaked small pieces of bread in the water. When Elenna had finished, Tom offered the food to the youth, who chewed hesitantly.

Silver and Storm came close, watching as Tom and Elenna did what they could to make the wounded boy comfortable.

"Who is he?" Elenna asked.

"There's a bag hanging from his saddle – that might give us a clue," said Tom.

A few moments later, Elenna was back with the bag. She rummaged inside.

"There's a lassoing rope and a triple sling for catching birds," she said. "Perhaps he's a cattle herder?" She looked at Tom. "Might he have something to do with that cattle pen we passed?"

Tom shook his head. "He's alone," he said. "Herders usually work in groups. He could be a rustler. People here seem willing to do anything to survive." He paused for a moment. "Still," he continued. "You take the sling and I'll keep the rope. They may come in useful."

Tom gazed off to the east. A slender ribbon of silvery light was just beginning to show over the distant hills.

"Dawn's coming," he said.

Elenna shivered. "But it's so cold! I wish we could build a fire."

"Even if we had wood and a tinder box, we'd be foolish to set a fire," said Tom, looping the rope over his shoulder. "Flames will draw the soldiers to us – and if that happens—"

Tom broke off at the sound of the youth's murmuring. "The great creature," he was saying, his face twisting in fear and pain. "The monster on the plains…"

Tom rested his hand on the youth's shoulder. "It's all right," he said. "The monster is gone."

The light grew slowly from the east. Tom stood on the hilltop, watching the horizon for the first glimpse of the sun. Silver was at his side, his head lifted as he sniffed for danger.

"What can you sense, boy?" Tom asked.

He scanned the landscape, but

no – he couldn't see anything suspicious. He walked back to where the youth lay with Elenna sitting close at hand.

"He seems a little more alert," she said. "He's talking about the monster again."

Suddenly Silver gave a low growl and went bounding down the hill.

"Silver, stop!" Elenna cried, jumping to her feet.

But the wolf ignored her. Tom saw that he was running towards a dense clump of tall grass fifty paces away.

"He's seen something," Tom said, stooping to pick up his spear. Elenna was at his side in a moment, the sword in her hand.

Silver was only a few paces from the patch of thick grass when there was a sudden flurry of movement.

Tom gasped as a great white shape burst from cover, leaping at Silver. It was twice the size of a wagon, and quicker than any horse Tom had ever seen.

"It's a cat-Beast!" cried Elenna.

The fearsome creature landed directly in front of the startled wolf. Its ferocious eyes were yellow, and its cruel claws jet-black. It opened its fanged jaws and let out a dreadful spitting hiss as its silvery white fur stood on end like spikes.

Madara had arrived!

CHAPTER SEVEN

BATTLING THE BEAST

Madara's black claws raked the ground, digging deep grooves in the earth. The Beast's huge yellow eyes looked from Tom to Elenna, full of malice and cunning.

Tom had to remind himself that this Beast was not evil – her rage was caused by being ripped from her natural home.

Calling on the power of the ruby jewel in his belt, Tom was able to understand the Beast's thoughts for a moment. He caught a fleeting glimpse of Madara's distress, trapped on the plains. She doesn't belong here, he thought. She's suffering, confused, and distressed to be torn away from her proper home in the chilly mountains.

With a howl, Silver flung himself at the monster cat. Madara reared up and with the swipe of a single paw, sent the brave wolf crashing head over heels into the grass.

Elenna let out a scream of alarm. Madara's fierce, blazing eyes turned to her and a moment later the Beast was bounding up the hillside towards them, her long, dagger-sharp teeth bared in a hideous grimace.

Tom snatched up his spear and sprang forwards. He knelt, ramming the butt of the spear into the ground and aiming the point at an angle towards the onrushing Beast.

He heard a frightened neigh behind him. From the corner of his eye he saw the wounded youth's horse bolting towards a gap in the stones.

Madara leaped away from Tom's spear, twisting in the air and landing to one side. She turned her head, terrifying eyes catching sight of the bolting horse that was cantering down the mountainside in panic.

A moment later, the Beast sprang away from Tom and pursued the horse in long loping bounds across the hillside.

"Tom!" called Elenna. "You must stop the Beast!"

But it was hopeless; Madara was already too far away for Tom to throw his spear. He raced after the Beast, but he had hardly gone four paces before the huge white cat caught up with the horse. Her black claws sank into the horse's back.

The horse's whinny of terror was brutally cut short by Madara's fangs

stabbing into its neck.

Tom pointed at the injured stranger. "Hide him!" he called to Elenna, who was casting a concerned glance towards Silver, lying on the ground and panting hard.

She ran towards the youth as Tom raced through the stones and leaped onto Storm's back, his spear gripped tightly in his fist.

He spurred Storm into a gallop. If he was quick, this might be the perfect moment to defeat Madara, while the huge cat was busy with her prey.

But the moment Madara saw Tom approaching, she jumped away from the dead horse and back onto flat ground, fangs dripping blood and eyes alight with rage.

Tom brought Storm to a halt,

watching the Beast and wondering if he should throw the spear in the hope of wounding her?

If he missed, he would be left defenceless.

I need to get in closer, he thought.

"Go, boy!" he shouted to Storm.

Storm charged towards the waiting monster. At the very last second, Madara bounded aside, but something strange happened as Tom came close to the Beast. She gave a great roar of anger and the white fur that bristled all over her body seemed to harden and become stiff as if it had turned into crystal.

Tom had only a fraction of time to act. As the Beast leaped aside, she exposed her flank to Tom's spear. He loosed his spear at Madara's hind legs. He knew the Beast was not evil at heart, and did not want to kill her. But he had to slow her down.

Tom gave a groan of dismay as his spear glanced off the hard white spikes, sending glassy splinters flying.

Madara roared, her claws reaching for Storm. Tom's horse twisted to avoid the blow, but lost his balance and stumbled. Tom was pitched headlong from the saddle.

He managed to curl into a roll. In a moment he was on his feet again.

"I don't give in so easily!" he shouted to the furious Beast.

But Storm was in trouble. Tom could see splinters of white glass in the horse's forelegs – the shards of Madara's deadly fur.

Running to Storm's side, he tried to draw out the splinters – but before he could, he heard a hissing sound behind him. Turning, he saw Madara looming over him.

The Beast's great yellow eyes stared down unblinkingly at him – Tom realized that Madara did not have eyelids. The Beast didn't blink – there would never be a moment when she could be taken unawares.

But Tom saw that his spear was within reach. Springing forwards, he snatched the spear up and thrust the point at the Beast. The fur no longer jutted out like glassy spikes – it was smooth, and she was vulnerable.

Why is it smooth again? he wondered. Perhaps Madara can't keep her fur hard for long. That may be her one weakness!

But as Tom moved in to strike, watchful for those deadly claws, Madara bounded away from the point of his spear. Landing lightly, the great cat pounced at Tom from the side, her jaws gaping and fangs dripping blood.

Tom swung his spear as the Beast bounded forwards. Madara swerved her body away from the point and snapped her teeth onto the spear's wooden shaft. With a single crunch, Tom's only weapon was shattered.

Tom jumped up onto a boulder. Using the broken end of the spear as a club, he struck the Beast a heavy blow on the head.

Hissing and shaking her head in pain, Madara backed away. But there was a determined light in her eyes. Tom had hurt the Beast, and now she was resolved to finish him off.

"Over here!" It was Elenna, racing down the hillside, banging the hilt of her sword against the shield, making plenty of noise to distract Madara.

With a yowling roar, Madara leaped to one side and went streaking up towards the stones. Leaving the injured Storm, Tom ran after the Beast. He still had the stranger's rope looped across his body. Unwinding it as he ran, he swung the lasso over his head.

"Keep Madara busy!" he shouted to Elenna as he closed in on the Beast from behind.

If he could lasso Madara and then hitch the end of the rope around one of the stones, the Beast would be trapped. While Elenna darted from side to side, brandishing her sword in the Beast's face, Tom swung the lasso twice more over his head and flung it at Madara.

For a joyful moment he thought the lasso would catch over her massive neck, but the fur turned to crystal again and the rope was cut to shreds, falling away.

Tom came to a stumbling halt – how could he fight a creature with such a formidable power?

Roaring, Madara leaped at him. Tom flung himself to the ground and the huge Beast went flying over his back.

He got to his feet again in time to see Madara bounding towards Elenna. She turned and ran, but it was hopeless. In two leaps, Madara had caught up with her.

Elenna tried to turn and fight, but she was beaten to the ground by the huge creature, which stood over her, hissing with furious intent.

"Elenna!" Tom yelled as he ran back down the hill. She was still wearing the chain mail they had taken from the soldiers, and Tom pinned all his hopes on that saving her from Madara's attack.

But before Tom even got within throwing distance, Madara's grotesque teeth clamped down on Elenna's shoulder and neck.

CHAPTER EIGHT

CAT AND MOUSE

Tom's heart was in his mouth as he
ran towards the dreadful scene. Was
Elenna dead?

No! He saw her struggling under
the weight of the monstrous cat.

The metal collar of the chainmail
jerkin had saved her from Madara's
teeth. But only just, Tom realised
with a shiver of unease. Elenna had
dropped her sword, and her shield

was dangling uselessly from her arm.

"Stay still!" Tom shouted as he approached the giant cat. Madara released Elenna from her vicious bite, holding her down with one huge paw.

Elenna stopped struggling.

Madara lowered her head again and caught Elenna's arm up in her jaws, half-dragging Tom's friend across the ground, towards a tall rock. Biting down on the chain mail, Madara pulled her up onto the rock.

The Beast lifted her head and let out a triumphant roar, front claws tearing at the rock, sending stone fragments flying. Elenna lay absolutely still between Madara's paws, playing dead. Madara thinks she's been killed, Tom thought. At least Elenna was safe – for now.

He picked up his friend's sword,
watching the Beast as it stood huge
and proud on the rock. He dived for
cover behind some boulders. From
this hiding place he stared up at the
creature. He saw a small patch of
bare skin on Madara's flank.

"That must be where my spear
broke the crystal fur," he murmured.
"But how can I take advantage
of that?"

His eye was caught by long morning shadows crawling across the plain as the sun rose in the east.

An idea struck him. Shadows!

He remembered the white diamond in his belt that he had won from Kaymon the Gorgon Hound. It gave him the power to separate his shadow from his body. There was only one drawback – while the shadow was loose, Tom was unable to move. But it would be worth the danger if he could use his shadow to draw Madara away from Elenna.

Tom concentrated hard. Slowly, he felt his shadow peeling away from him. It crouched at his side, waiting for his instructions.

He pointed to the huge cat. "Make her chase you down off the rock," he said. "Go!"

With a single nod, the shadow went leaping out into the open, running this way and that under the rock, jumping into the air and throwing its arms up.

Madara stared down, confused. She growled and scraped her claws along the rock.

Undaunted, the shadow sauntered away. The Beast stared after it, with her head low and her hindquarters raised up. Her tail lashed furiously at the rock.

Finally, with a yowling roar, Madara leapt forwards.

She came to a tumbling halt as the flighty shadow flitted away, out of reach. Yowling with anger, the Beast pounced again and again, but each time Tom's shadow danced out of reach.

Madara's yowls were now roars and snarls of frustrated fury. No matter how quickly the claws swiped, the prancing shape always managed to slip free.

Up on the rock, Tom noticed Elenna gingerly pushing herself up. This was her chance to escape! She scrambled down the rock, running to where Tom crouched, unable to move while his shadow taunted the Beast.

"Call it back now," Elenna told him. "You're helpless without it."

Tom stared at his shadow, willing the dark shape to return to him. With a final flying leap, the shadow sprang out from under Madara's latest attack and raced towards Tom.

The Beast chased after it, eyes burning with hatred.

For a moment, Tom was afraid that Madara would reach him before the shadow did.

But in the nick of time, the shadow jumped over the rocks and slipped back beside Tom, making his body shudder as they were reunited.

Madara was only a heartbeat behind. Elenna braced her shield against the Beast as they jumped to one side.

Madara landed between them, turning her head from side to side as she tried to decide which of these creatures she would kill first.

"Tom, catch!" Elenna called, tossing him her sword.

Madara lunged at Tom's friend. Elenna just managed to bring her shield up to block the gaping fangs.

Now the Beast spun and attacked Tom, forcing him to dodge aside, sword ringing as it bounced off the white glass of the Beast's crystal fur.

Tom ducked as the Beast's jaws snapped dangerously close to his sword arm. His blade rattled on the long sharp fangs and he felt Madara's breath blasting into his face. Tom somersaulted to avoid slashing claws, his sword a blur of light as he fought to keep the monster at bay.

The creature's unblinking eyes glared at him as she reared up, clawing at him again and again. She seemed tireless.

How long can I keep this up? Tom thought, his muscles straining. *One swipe of those claws, and I'll be dead.*

CHAPTER NINE

SPLINTERS

A howl sounded from behind Tom. He glanced over his shoulder.

Silver!

The brave wolf was alive – but as he loped forwards, Tom could see that he was far from steady on his feet. Madara's earlier attack had severely weakened him.

"No!" Elenna cried. "Keep back, Silver! She'll cut you to pieces!"

The wolf ran to stand close to her, snarling and baring his teeth.

"We have to smash the fur!" Tom shouted to Elenna. "It's the only way to make the Beast vulnerable."

In the few moments it took to call to Elenna, Madara was upon Tom in a flurry of teeth and claws. Tom's sword struck off the black claws as he leaped high to avoid a raking swipe.

Tom saw that Elenna had taken out the sling she'd found in the wounded stranger's bag. Now, she was crouching and scooping up stones.

"Over here!" Tom yelled, waving his sword and running around so that Madara's attention was drawn away from Elenna.

Madara yowled in rage. The Beast's hackle's rose up, the fur becoming glassy shards again. The claws slashed, missing Tom by a hair's-breadth as he dove to the ground. He rolled quickly away as the open jaws came down to bite through his flesh and bone. *Smash!*

Madara spun around with a roar of anger. Elenna had slung a stone with all her might, and it had smashed and broken some of the Beast's fur. Again she spun the sling and threw.

Another stone shattered splinters of glass from the great cat's haunch.

Now Tom could see a patch of bare skin. Elenna's attack was working!

While the Beast's attention was on Elenna, Tom leaped forwards, bringing his sword down on Madara's flank. He winced as flying shards grazed his cheek. Quick as lightning, Madara turned on him, spitting with pain and rage. *Smash!*

Another of Elenna's stones struck his glassy fur. *Slash!*

Tom's sword struck the Beast's shoulder, cutting away more spikes.

Eyes blazing with dreadful fury and jaws wide open, Madara flung herself at Tom. He just managed to sidestep the razor-sharp fangs as the Beast hurtled past. There was a loud crash and the air rained white crystals.

Madara had crashed head first into a rock. The Beast staggered, legs buckling as she tried to turn again. Sharp pieces of fur had broken away from her forehead, and Tom saw that the lidless eyes were dazed.

Lifting his sword, Tom leapt up at the Beast. He brought the swordhilt down between Madara's eyes.

The great cat's legs gave and she went sprawling onto her side. Her tongue lolled and her flanks rapidly rose and fell as she breathed.

Tom stood over the Beast, sword poised. He could kill her at any moment. "I won't do that," he said.

Madara's wide unblinking eyes seemed to soften. A whirling roar filled Tom's ears – a noise like a great sucking wind. He stepped back as Madara was lifted from the ground and swept up into the morning sky.

For a few moments Tom saw the Beast glowing in the sunlight far above, then she was pulled towards the portal. Madara grew smaller as the cyclone bore her up into the seething slash in the sky. Then the fading white shape was gone, amid a deafening clap of thunder that seemed to shake the whole kingdom.

The portal spat billowing clouds that blotted out all light. Tom watched, astounded and terrified.

He couldn't see anything!

"Tom!" Elenna shouted in the blackness. "What's going on?"

White lightning tore through the blackness. In the space of two heartbeats, the clouds rolled away and bright morning sunlight washed over the plains. Tom heard Elenna give a whoop of joy. Silver was barking and Storm whinnied.

Tom lowered his sword, smiling as he stared up into the sky. Madara had been returned to her rightful home in the mountains, wherever that might be in the kingdom – back to the place she was destined to protect. Elenna appeared at his side.

"Why hasn't anything of Oradu's been sent down to us?" she asked "Is something wrong?"

Was the Quest still not over?

CHAPTER TEN

SURRENDER

"The Beast returning home seemed different this time," Elenna said. "But you saved Madara – that's the main thing."

Tom wasn't so sure. "Perhaps you're right," he said. "How's the wounded boy?"

"I pulled him out of sight behind some rocks," said Elenna. "We should go check on him."

First, Tom went to Storm. With gentle fingers he pulled the shards of Madara's glassy fur from his forelegs. Fortunately, the gallant stallion was not seriously hurt. As if to show Tom that everything was all right, he nudged Tom with his nose and whinnied softly. Silver rubbed up against him, also recovered from his encounter with Madara.

Tom smiled as he looked at his two animal friends – as hard as it had been to defeat this Beast, things could have been far worse.

Storm and Silver followed along behind as Tom and Elenna made their way back onto the ridge of standing stones.

The youth seemed less feverish now, but he was still too weak to stand. Tom knelt at his side and checked his wounds.

"Can you ride, do you think?" Elenna asked the youth.

He looked at them with dazed eyes and shook his head. "Must...sleep..." he murmured.

"Yes, that's fine," Tom said, standing up. "You sleep now." He looked at Elenna. "We'll stay here until he's fit to move," he said. "Then we'll take him somewhere to be looked after properly."

"And what about afterwards?" Elenna asked. "Where do we go next? And don't forget, we have an entire army searching for us."

"I haven't forgotten," Tom said.

The shrill cry of a bird caught his attention. He looked up at the skies.

"Look!" he cried, pointing to the eastern horizon. A dark shape was

winging its way towards them.

"What kind of bird is that?" asked
Elenna, shielding her eyes.

"I think it's a falcon," said Tom.

The magnificent grey bird fluttered
in to land on top of one of the stones.
It gave a single cry and stared down
at them.

Tom stepped up to the rock. "Who
sent you?" he said, understanding
that this was no ordinary bird.

His hands clenched into fists. "Are you some minion of Malvel's?"

The bird stared down at Tom, its eyes glittering, black as ebony. Then it looked away to where Storm was standing, and gave a single cry.

Tom turned. Storm's saddlebag flew open and Oradu's cloak, staff and hat flew out. They twirled together in the air, growing to their correct size. Then they floated down, the cloak taking on the Good Wizard's shape, with the hat hanging above. Oradu appeared, ghostly but recognizable, clutching the staff, his eyes burning under his brows.

The falcon gave another cry and launched itself into the air. As Tom and Elenna watched, the bird circled the wizard twice and then came to settle on his outstretched arm.

"The falcon is the next token!" gasped Tom.

"You have done well, my friends," came Oradu's spectral voice. "The fourth Beast has been guided home, and a fourth portal has been closed."

"What is our next Quest, Oradu?" asked Tom.

"Your next task may be the hardest you have ever undertaken," said the wizard. "You must..."

But before he could finish speaking, he turned his head, staring at something behind Tom and Elenna.

A moment later, the pale form evaporated like mist and the cloak and hat and staff fell lifelessly to the ground. With an alarmed cry, the falcon took to the air and went skimming away to the east.

"What happened?" cried Elenna.

"Where's Oradu gone?"

"I don't know," said Tom, staring at the wizard's empty clothes.

A growl from Silver made the two friends turn.

"It's them, for sure!" snarled a familiar voice. It was Nathan, the man they had left bound and gagged out on the plain. Climbing the hill with him were Peter and at least a dozen soldiers, all armed.

Tom's fingers closed instinctively on his sword hilt. But there were too many soldiers for him to fight. Already they were surrounded and hemmed in by pikes and swords and deadly looking crossbows.

Tom let go of his sword and lifted his hands. "We will surrender," he said. "Although we've done nothing but good for your kingdom!"

"Nothing but good, is it?" growled Nathan, stepping forwards and gripping Tom's wrist. "See this? There's blood on his hands."

"And there's his victim!" said Peter, pointing to where the wounded youth lay.

"No, you don't understand," cried Elenna. "We were helping him. It was the Beast!"

"What Beast?" scoffed Nathan. "We can see no Beast around here!" He stared coldly into Tom's face. "We will need to add attempted murder to the charge of treason."

"I'm no murderer!" shouted Tom, trying to pull free of Nathan's pitiless grasp.

"Not another word, boy, or I'll execute you where you stand!" Nathan snarled. "And that goes for

the girl, too! One more word from either of you will mean death!"

Tom stared into the man's angry face. He and Elenna were friendless in a strange kingdom, surrounded by desperate enemies under the thrall of an evil king.

Tom turned in despair and looked at Elenna.

This time, surely, their Beast Quest was at its end.

Here's a sneak preview of Tom's
next exciting adventure!

Meet

ELLiK
THE LIGHTNING
HORROR

Only Tom can save Tavania from the
rule of the Evil Wizard Malvel...

PROLOGUE

Barbo the monkey sat high up in the branches of the Misty Jungle, swinging her furry brown tail.

Barbo lifted her nose and sniffed. She could smell ripe fruit nearby. Chattering softly to herself, she slipped off her branch and hung upside-down by her tail. Almost at once, she spotted the fruit on a neighbouring tree. She reached out and plucked a round, ripe papaya. Still hanging upside down, she bit into it and sucked hungrily at the juice.

On other branches, the rest of the monkey troop was also feeding.

Barbo finished her papaya and dropped the skin. She pulled herself the right way round. A star fruit twinkled temptingly, just out of reach. She sprang across two branches and pulled the succulent fruit from its nest of leaves.

As she was eating, Barbo saw her sister Chiro swinging towards her. The two monkeys greeted each other, grunting affectionately. Chiro began to comb through Barbo's fur, hunting for fleas. Feeling full and contented, Barbo settled down on a wide branch and started to doze.

A fizzing, crackling sound down on the jungle floor made her eyes snap open. The other monkeys shrieked in alarm, racing nimbly along the branches with their tails streaking behind them. Through the canopy of leaves, Barbo saw dark clouds roll across the sky.

Follow this Quest to the end in ELLIK THE LIGHTNING HORROR.

Win an exclusive
Beast Quest T-shirt and goody bag!

Tom has battled many fearsome Beasts and we want to know which one is your favourite! Send us a drawing or painting of your favourite Beast and tell us in 30 words why you think it's the best.

Each month we will select **three** winners to receive a Beast Quest T-shirt and goody bag!

Send your entry on a postcard to
BEAST QUEST COMPETITION
Orchard Books, 338 Euston Road, London NW1 3BH.

Australian readers should email:
childrens.books@hachette.com.au

New Zealand readers should write to:
Beast Quest Competition, 4 Whetu Place, Mairangi Bay,
Auckland NZ, or email: childrensbooks@hachette.co.nz

**Don't forget to include your name and address.
Only one entry per child.**

Good luck!

Join the Quest,
Join the Tribe

www.beastquest.co.uk

Have you checked out the Beast Quest website?
It's the place to go for games, downloads, activities,
sneak previews and lots of fun!

You can read all about your favourite Beasts, down-
load free screensavers and desktop wallpapers for
your computer, and even challenge your friends
to a Beast Tournament.

Sign up to the newsletter at www.beastquest.co.uk
to receive exclusive extra content and the oppor-
tunity to enter special members-only competitions.
We'll send you up-to-date info on all the Beast
Quest books, including the next exciting series
which features six brand-new Beasts!

Get 30% off all Beast Quest Books at www.beastquest.co.uk
Enter the code BEAST at the checkout.

Offer valid in UK and ROI, offer expires December 2013

All books priced at £4.99,
special bumper editions
priced at £5.99.

Orchard Books are available from all good bookshops, or
can be ordered from our website:
www.orchardbooks.co.uk,
or telephone 01235 827702, or fax 01235 8227703.

FREE COLLECTOR CARDS INSIDE!

Series 7: THE LOST WORLD
COLLECT THEM ALL!

Can Tom save the chaotic land of Tavania from dark Wizard Malvel's evil plans?

978 1 40830 729 8

978 1 40830 730 4

978 1 40830 731 1

978 1 40830 732 8

978 1 40830 733 5

978 1 40830 734 2

The Chronicles of Avantia

FROM THE DARK, A HERO ARISES...

Dare to enter the kingdom of Avantia.

A dark land, where wild creatures roam and people fight tooth-and-nail to survive another day.

And now, as the prophecies warned, a new evil arises. Lord Derthsin – power-hungry and driven by hatred – has ordered his armies into the four corners of Avantia. Just one flicker of hope remains...

If the four Beasts of Avantia can find their Chosen Riders – and unite them into a deadly fighting force – they might have the strength to challenge Derthsin. But if they fail, the land of Avantia will be lost forever...

FIRST HERO – OUT NOW!
Book two, CHASING EVIL, out in October 2010, with more great books to enjoy in 2011.

www.chroniclesofavantia.com